This book belongs

to ....

....

Text and illustrations copyright © 1987
Award Publications Limited
This 1987 edition published by Derrydale Books,
distributed by Crown Publishers, Inc.,
225 Park Avenue South, New York,
New York 10003

Printed in Hungary

ISBN 0-517-65071-1

MY BIG BOOK OF BRER RABBIT STORIES

Illustrated by

RENE CLOKE

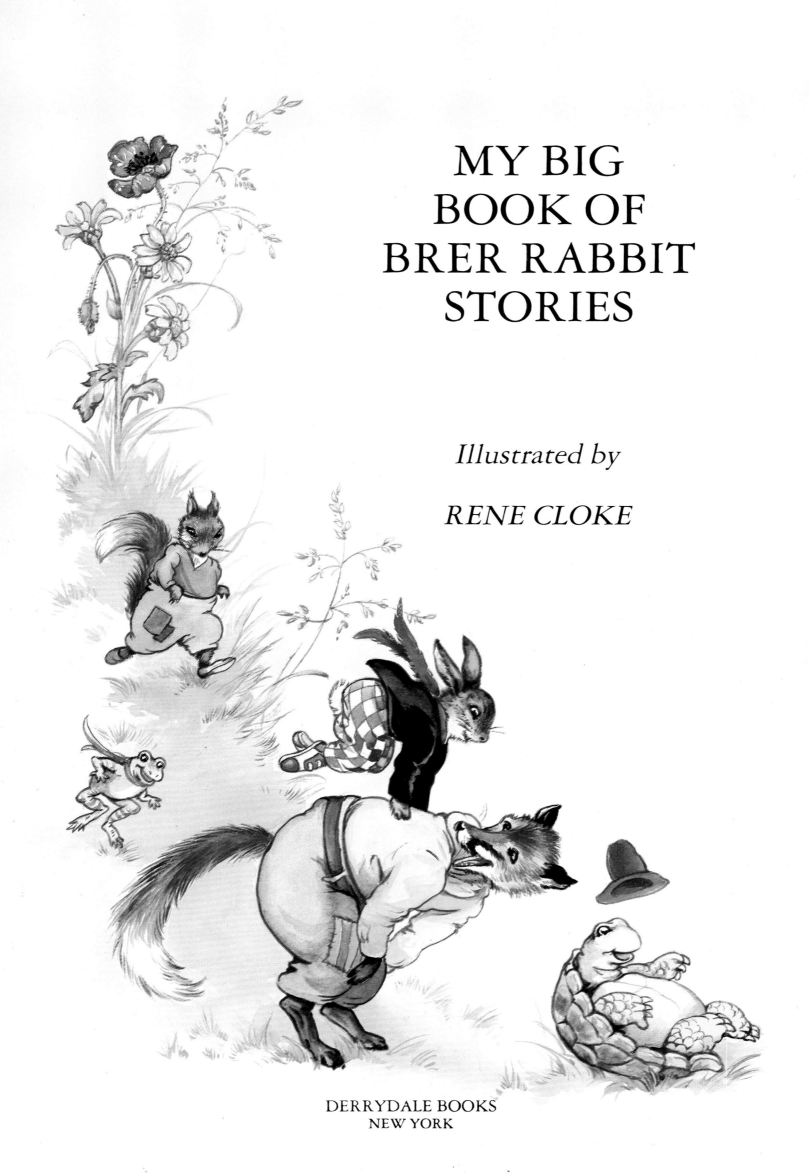

DERRYDALE BOOKS
NEW YORK

BRER TERRAPIN SHOWS HIS STRENGTH

One day when the animals were feeling quite friendly towards each other, they started talking about the wonderful things they could do.

"I can run the fastest," boasted Brer Rabbit.

"And I am the sharpest," said Brer Fox.

"But I am certainly the strongest," said great big Brer Bear. He certainly looked the strongest, although he didn't move as quickly as some of the others.

Brer Terrapin thought for a little while. He wasn't very big, but he was quite cunning and he tried to think of a way to show off.

At last he said, "I think I can
show you all that I am stronger
even than Brer Bear!"

This made the other animals laugh.

"How ridiculous!" declared Brer Bear
and Brer Fox.

But Brer Rabbit felt sure that Brer Terrapin was going to
play a trick.

"Bring a strong rope and we'll go to the river," answered
Brer Terrapin. "Then, see if Brer Bear can pull me out!"

So off they went.

When they reached the river, Brer Terrapin handed one end of the rope to Brer Bear.

"Take hold of that end," he said, "and walk away into the wood. I will hold this end and call out when you are to pull."

When they had gone out of sight,
Brer Terrapin dived into the river and
tied his end of the rope to the root of a
tree under the water.

Then he climbed out.

"Now pull!" he called to Brer Bear.

Brer Bear gave a little pull. He had hoped to pull the rope from Brer Terrapin very easily, but to his surprise it didn't move. So, he wrapped the rope around his paw and pulled harder, but still the rope didn't move.

"Pull harder!" called Brer Terrapin, jerking the rope.

Then Brer Bear put the rope over his shoulder and tugged and tugged, but he couldn't move it.

Next, all the animals tugged
together, but still Brer Terrapin sat
by the river holding the rope.
     At last he called, "Come back,
I'm tired of waiting."

As soon as he heard the others coming back, he dived into the river, untied the rope and sat on the river bank waiting for them.

"You tried hard," he said, "but you must agree that I'm just a bit stronger than you all!"

BRER RABBIT GOES SHOPPING

Brer Rabbit had such a good crop of corn that he decided to sell it and buy some of the things that Mrs. Rabbit was always asking for.

"We need tin plates and tin cups for the children," she told him, "and a new tin teapot."

So Brer Rabbit set off for market the next day.

"I've heard that Brer Rabbit is going to market to sell his corn," Brer Fox told his friends, Brer Wolf and Brer Bear. "Let's lie in wait for him and punish him for all the tricks he has played on us."

So they hid behind some trees by the roadside and waited.

Brer Rabbit soon caught sight of them.
He tied all the tin plates and cups around
his neck and the tin teapot on his head.
Then, with a great cry, he dashed down
the road.

"Here comes the tinker!" he yelled,
clashing the plates together. "I'm the iron
man - look out for my iron teeth!"
Brer Fox, Brer Wolf and Brer Bear were
terrified and ran off, leaving Brer Rabbit to
make his way safely home.

BRER RABBIT MEETS HIS MATCH

Brer Rabbit and Brer Buzzard decided to sow some seed and then to share the vegetable crop when it grew.

But when the time came for sharing out, there were no vegetables in the plot. As there was a very sly look on Brer Rabbit's face, Brer Buzzard felt sure Brer Rabbit had hidden them.

Brer Buzzard went away and thought very hard. The next day he called in to see Brer Rabbit.

"I've discovered a gold mine on the other side of the river," he said. "Come with me and we'll dig out the gold and share it."

"But how am I to cross the river?" asked Brer Rabbit.

"I'll carry you on my back," said Brer Buzzard, so Brer Rabbit scrambled up and off they went.

Instead of crossing the
water, Brer Buzzard perched
high up in a very tall tree in the
middle of the river.

Brer Rabbit didn't like this,
but Brer Buzzard kept laughing
and shaking until Brer Rabbit
was afraid he would fall off.

"Tell me where you have
hidden all the vegetables we grew,"
demanded Brer Buzzard, "then
we'll go back and divide them."
So Brer Rabbit had to agree and
they flew back to his garden and shared the crop of
vegetables he had hidden in his hut. But Brer Rabbit's
knees shook with fright for a long time afterwards.

BRER RABBIT AND BRER LION

Most small animals were very frightened when a lion came to live near their homes.

"He says he must have three good meals a day," said Brer Fox, shivering to the tip of his tail.

"I'm not frightened," declared Brer Rabbit. "I'll finish off Brer Lion."

He went to the pond, wet his fur and rolled in the mud until he looked a miserable object.

Next, he crawled up to Brer Lion's den.

"I'm your three meals for today," he told him. "The other lion wants all the sheep and bullocks."

"Does he indeed?" roared Brer Lion. "Just lead me to him and we'll fight it out!"

So Brer Rabbit took him to the well near by and peeping in he cried...

"He's very fierce and angry! Don't go near him!"

When Brer Lion rushed to the well and looked in the water, he saw his own angry face and thought it was another lion.

"I'll fight you!" he cried. "We'll soon see who has the better meals!"

He dived in and was drowned and that was the end of Brer Lion.

"That's the way to deal with lions!" said Brer Rabbit.

BRER RABBIT'S RIDING HORSE

Brer Rabbit was visiting the Possum family and having a little chat. As usual, he couldn't help making fun of Brer Fox.

"My father used to ride Brer Fox for years," he boasted. "He was quite a good riding horse."

Of course, the Possums laughed at this joke.

"We don't believe it," they said. "Show us how he did it!"

So Brer Rabbit made his plans.

When Brer Fox passed his door next day, he called out…

"Please help me, Brer Fox. I want to go to the Possum's party but I've hurt my foot. May I ride on your back?"

Brer Fox thought that
this would be a good chance
to give Brer Rabbit a rough
time, so he agreed and
dressed himself in a saddle,
bridle and reins.

Off they went.
They rode along quietly for a little while before Brer Fox
asked, "Why are you wriggling, Brer Rabbit?"
    "Just shortening the stirrups a little," answered
Brer Rabbit, with a sly grin.

He was really putting on
a pair of sharp spurs. Then,
when they came to the
Possum's house, where Brer
Fox had meant to toss Brer
Rabbit to the ground, Brer
Rabbit gave a dig of the
spurs to make Brer Fox
gallop up the path in fine
style.

Brer Rabbit jumped off and tied Brer Fox to the railings before
he could take his revenge.
    Brer Rabbit walked up to the astonished Possum family.
    "I told you he was a good riding horse," he said to them.
"He will be better still when I've trained him a little!"

BRER FOX TRICKED AGAIN

When it was time to go home, Brer Rabbit untied Brer Fox and leaped onto his back. This time, Brer Fox was ready for him.

As soon as they reached the wood, Brer Fox rolled over and over on his back until Brer Rabbit fell off.

His spurs were no use to him now, so off he scampered into the wood.

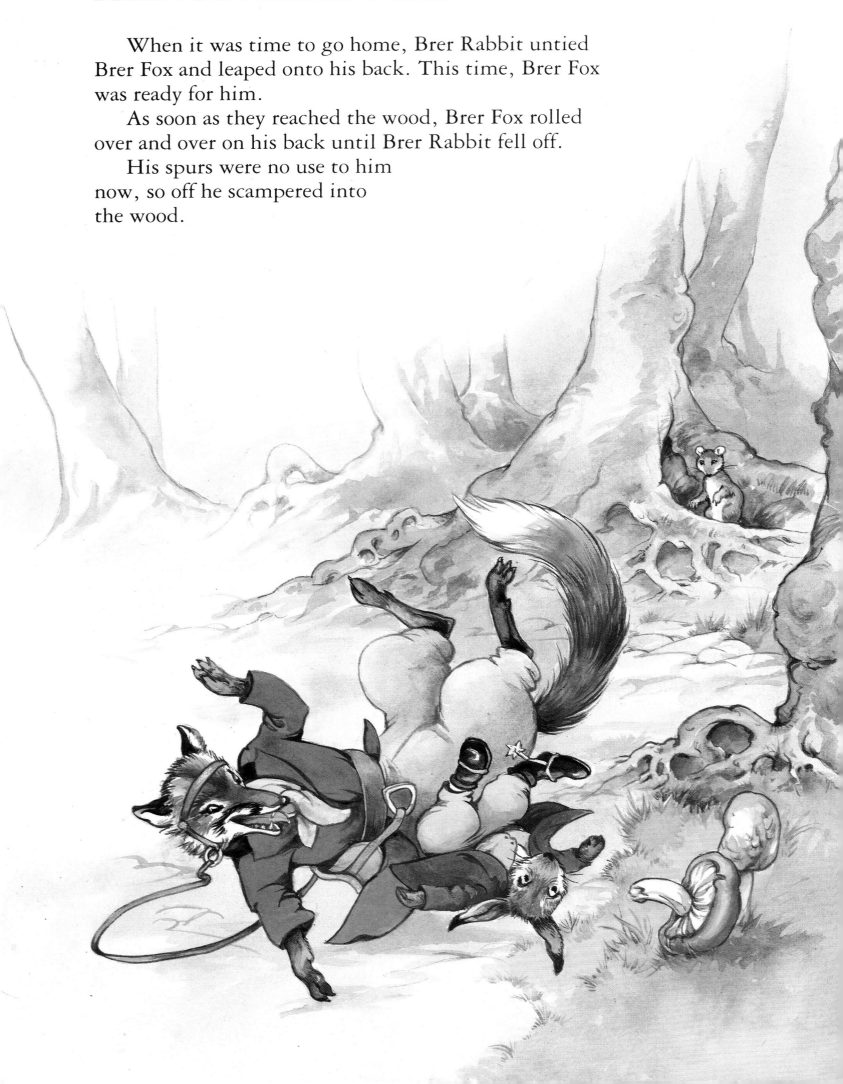

By the time Brer Fox
was on his feet, Brer
Rabbit was disappearing
inside a hollow tree.

Brer Fox ran after
him, but the hole was
too small for him. He lay
down and tried to think
what to do next.

"Hello!" said Brer Buzzard
walking by. "What are you doing?"

"I've got Brer Rabbit in this
tree," answered Brer Fox. "Will
you watch him while I fetch my axe
to chop down the tree?"

So Brer Buzzard sat and waited.

Brer Rabbit had heard the talk and he called out,

"If Brer Buzzard was here he could catch a fat squirrel for
his dinner. I could chase it out of the tree on the other side."
Then he scratched away to make Brer Buzzard
think he was chasing the squirrel.

When Brer Buzzard ran around the tree, Brer
Rabbit dashed out of the hole and ran for home.

When Brer Fox came
back with his axe and found
that Brer Rabbit had
escaped, he was furious.

"I'll throw you on the fire!" he shouted at Brer
Buzzard. He grabbed his tail, but the feathers came
out and Brer Buzzard was able to fly away.
"Tricked again!" groaned Brer Fox.
And Brer Rabbit had a good laugh
at them both.

BRER RABBIT AND BRER FOX

Brer Rabbit was a naughty little fellow. He liked to play tricks on Brer Fox, Brer Wolf and the other animals who were always trying to catch him.

But Brer Rabbit was so clever that he managed to escape every time and went on playing his tricks.

One day, Brer Wolf and Brer Fox decided to put a stop to this so they made a plan.

"I've thought of a good idea," said Brer Wolf, "run home, get into bed and pretend to be dead and I will go to Brer Rabbit's house with the news. When Brer Rabbit comes to look at you, just jump up and catch him!"

"That should be easy," agreed Brer Fox and he trotted home and went to bed.

As soon as Brer Fox had gone, Brer Wolf went along to Brer Rabbit's house and called out —

"Are you there, Brer Rabbit? Sad news, poor Brer Fox died this morning. I'm just going around to tell his friends," and off he ran.

When the wolf had gone, Brer Rabbit sat down and thought hard.

"This sounds like a trick," he said and decided to go to Brer Fox's house and see for himself if the fox was really dead.

When he got to Brer Fox's house, he walked carefully around to see if any traps were set and then he peeped into the window.

There was Brer Fox, lying on the bed, with his eyes shut so Brer Rabbit went to the open door.

"Poor Brer Fox," he said aloud. "I wonder if he is really dead? I think he must be for he lies very still, I had better wait here until his friends come."

Then he had another look at Brer Fox.

"You can always tell when a fox is dead," he said, "because he keeps shaking his left leg."

When Brer Fox heard this, he thought he had better shake his leg but, of course, as soon as he did this, Brer Rabbit knew that he was just pretending.

He dashed out of the house and didn't stop running until he was safely home.

"They can't catch me with that trick," he laughed.

And he went on laughing all the time he was having his tea.

THE TAR BABY

Brer Fox tried to think of a good way to catch Brer Rabbit but the rabbit was always too clever for him.

One day, Brer Fox worked out a new plan.

With a lot of tar he made a tar-baby, put a hat on its head and stuck it on a stick near Brer Rabbit's house; then he hid in some bushes and waited to see what would happen.

Before long, Brer Rabbit came walking by and, when he saw the tar-baby, he stopped and looked at it in surprise. He had never seen anything quite like that before.

"Good morning," said Brer Rabbit, "it's a fine day."

But the tar-baby didn't answer. "Can't you hear me?" shouted Brer Rabbit at the top of his voice.

But still the tar-baby didn't answer.

This made Brer Rabbit so angry that he rushed up and hit the tar-baby and, of course, his paw stuck to the tar.

"Let go," yelled Brer Rabbit, "or I'll hit you again!"

So he hit out with his other paws and those stuck as well.

There was Brer Rabbit stuck to the tar-baby and he couldn't get off.

Then Brer Fox walked out from the bushes and laughed, for this was just what he had hoped would happen.

"You seem to be stuck up this morning, Brer Rabbit" he said. "Now I've caught you at last and I mean to punish you. You won't play any more tricks on me!"

Brer Rabbit thought quickly.

"Do what you like with me, Brer Fox," he cried, "but don't throw me into the briar patch! Hang me or drown me but, *please*, don't throw me into the briar patch!"

"That must be the best way to hurt him," thought Brer Fox, so he pulled Brer Rabbit from the tar-baby and flung him into the briar patch.

"That will be the end of him!" he barked.

But, in a moment, Brer Rabbit had scrambled out.

"I was born and bred in a briar patch!" he laughed as he scampered home. "Born and bred in a briar patch!"

BRER RABBIT AND BRER TORTOISE

When Brer Rabbit was out one day, he saw Brer Fox hustling along with a sack over his shoulder. He seemed to be in a great hurry.

Something was kicking and shouting inside the sack.

"That sounds like someone I know," said Brer Rabbit. "I believe it's Brer Tortoise."

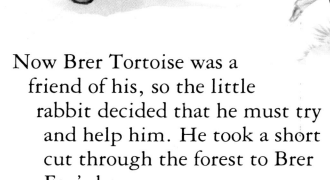

Now Brer Tortoise was a friend of his, so the little rabbit decided that he must try and help him. He took a short cut through the forest to Brer Fox's house.

When he got there, he ran into the garden and tore up a lot of plants from the flower beds.

Then he hid by the front door.

After a time, Brer Fox appeared with the sack over his shoulder and Brer Rabbit called out, "Fetch a big stick, Brer Fox! Someone is tearing up plants in your garden!"

Dropping the sack on the doorstep, Brer Fox took up a stick and rushed into the garden.

While he was searching for the rascal, Brer Rabbit undid the sack and let out his friend Brer Tortoise.

Then, between them, they took one of Brer Fox's beehives and stuffed it into the sack.

"That will give him a surprise!" whispered Brer Rabbit as they tied up the sack and put it back on the doorstep.

Brer Fox came back from the garden feeling very angry because he couldn't find anyone pulling up his plants. He picked up the sack and went into his house, slamming the door behind him.

Brer Rabbit and Brer Tortoise sat in the bushes and waited.

Then they heard a great noise of buzzing and yelping, and out ran Brer Fox with the angry bees buzzing around him and stinging him as he ran.

"I thought I had captured a tortoise in my sack!" howled Brer Fox. "How can I have made such a mistake?"

"Ha, ha!" laughed Brer Rabbit, "that will teach him to leave tortoises alone — they might turn into a hive of bees!"

The two friends hurried off before Brer Fox discovered that they had tricked him.

BRER RABBIT AND
BRER FOX GO FISHING

One very hot day, all the animals were digging a patch of ground together so that they could plant some vegetables.

As Brer Rabbit was rather small, he found it hard work and after a time he threw down his fork and called out, "I've got a thorn in my paw, I must stop and pull it out."

He walked off to a shady spot and pretended to get the thorn from his paw.

Then he saw, a little way off, a well with a bucket hanging from it. "How cool that looks!" thought Brer Rabbit, "I'll hop into that bucket and have a nap."

But as soon as he stepped into the bucket,
it started going down the well.

"Ho! ho!" gasped Brer Rabbit, "where am
I going?"

Down, down went the bucket; the well was dark and cold and
when, at last, the bucket hit the water the rabbit, very frightened,
wondered what to do next.

Brer Fox had been watching Brer Rabbit and, thinking he was up
to a trick, he followed him into the wood. He saw him jump into
the bucket and disappear.

"That's a funny thing to do," he muttered. "I wonder if Brer Rabbit keeps all his money down there?"

He peeped into the well and saw Brer Rabbit sitting in the bucket in the water.

"What are you doing down there?" he called to him.

"Oh, I'm fishing," replied Brer Rabbit. "I thought some fish would be a nice surprise for dinner for us all."

"Are there many down there?" asked Brer Fox, peering into the well.

"Oh, yes! Dozens and dozens of them!" answered Brer Rabbit. "Come and help me and we'll soon have enough for everyone."

"How can I get down?" the fox asked him.

"Just get into the other bucket," said Brer Rabbit. "That will bring you down."

Brer Rabbit seemed to be having a very good time and, as Brer Fox was fond of fish, he decided to join him.

Although he was rather big for the bucket, he managed to creep into it.

But, of course, he was much heavier than the little rabbit and, as his bucket went down, Brer Rabbit's bucket came up.

"Catch a nice bucketful of fish, Brer Fox!" cried Brer Rabbit as the buckets passed each other. "It's nice and cool down there!"

It was a long time before someone helped Brer Fox out of the well and, by that time, Brer Rabbit had run home.

THE GREAT RACE

Brer Rabbit was very good at playing tricks on the other animals but sometimes they were too clever for him.

Brer Terrapin was walking slowly along the road one day when he met Brer Rabbit.

"Hello slow poke!" laughed Brer Rabbit. "You look as though you're in a hurry!"

Brer Terrapin felt annoyed.

"I may be slow on land," he replied, "but I'm a good swimmer."

Brer Rabbit knew that although Brer Terrapin could swim, he was no quicker in the water than he was on the land.

"We'll have a race," said Brer Rabbit. "I'll go by land and you can swim in the river." Brer Terrapin agreed to this, so all the animals helped them to measure five miles along the river path, marking each mile with a post.

Early next morning, Brer Terrapin put his wife and each of his four children at a post, then hid himself at the winning post.

All the terrapins looked the same, so when Mrs. Terrapin dived into the water at the words

"Ready? Go!" Brer Rabbit thought that she was Brer Terrapin.

He was surprised to see a terrapin swimming away from each mile post as he reached it. "I didn't think Brer Terrapin could swim so fast!" he panted.

When he reached the winning post, he was amazed to find Brer Terrapin already there. "I'm tired of waiting for you," laughed the terrapin. "Did you lose your way?"

Brer Rabbit simply couldn't understand what had happened.

How had Brer Terrapin arrived first at the winning post when he was such a slow poke?

But he was careful not to laugh at the terrapin next time he met him crawling along.

BRER FOX GOES HUNTING

Brer Fox went hunting one day and came back in the evening with a heavy bag over his shoulder. He didn't know that Brer Rabbit was watching him from the bushes.

"There must be something good in that bag," said Brer Rabbit to himself. "Perhaps I can trick Brer Fox into giving some of it to me. I would like a tasty morsel for my supper."

He ran on ahead of Brer Fox, pulled off his clothes and lay down in the middle of the road, pretending to be dead.

Along came Brer Fox who turned over the rabbit with his stick.

"Here's a fine fat rabbit," he declared, "and he seems to be dead. A pity I can't take him but I've as much as I can carry already," and off he went.

As soon as Brer Fox
was out of sight,
Brer Rabbit jumped up
and, running through
the woods, he lay down
again in the road where
he knew Brer Fox would
find him.

"Well, this is a surprise," said Brer Fox,
looking at the rabbit. "Another dead rabbit
just waiting to be picked up. I think I'll
leave my bag here and go back and
collect the other one. It seems
silly not to have them both.

I'll bring another
bag to put them in."

Off went Brer Fox
thinking of the fine
feast he would have;
a bagful of birds
and animals, and two
fat rabbits as well.

"Just as I planned," laughed Brer
Rabbit jumping up and putting on his
clothes as soon as Brer Fox had
disappeared down the road.
He snatched up the bag
and trotted home with it.
"Tricked again!" growled Brer Fox
when he discovered that the two
dead rabbits had vanished
as well as his bag and he
had to go home without
any supper.

HOW BRER RABBIT LOST HIS TAIL

Many years ago, Brer Rabbit had a long bushy tail rather like a squirrel. He was very proud of it and used to shake it as he walked.

One bright winter morning he met Brer Fox walking along carrying a string of fine fish.

"Those look good," said Brer Rabbit. "Where did you catch them?"

"I caught them down in the river," answered Brer Fox.
"There are plenty there."

"How did you catch them?" asked Brer Rabbit.

Brer Fox sat down on a log and tried to think for a
moment how he could play a trick on Brer Rabbit.

"All you have to do," he said,
"is to drop your tail into the
water in the evening and, when
you draw it up in the morning,
it will be covered with fish."

"It sounds easy," thought Brer Rabbit.

So, that evening he put on his big warm coat and muffler, packed a basket of food and a hot drink, and set off to fish.

He sat on a big stone in the river and let his tail down into the water.

It was very, very cold and by morning poor Brer Rabbit felt quite frozen.

"I must be catching a fine lot of fish," he said to cheer himself up.

But when he tried to pull his tail out of the water, he found that it had frozen and as he got up, it snapped off! "Well, that was a trick," moaned poor Brer Rabbit looking at his stump of fluffy tail, "and no fish!"

And that is why rabbits now have little bob tails.

BRER RABBIT AND BRER BEAR

Brer Rabbit was very fond of green peas and lettuce and, when he found them growing in Brer Fox's garden, he crawled through the fence every day and had a good feast.

"I must set a trap", said Brer Fox, "someone is stealing my green peas and lettuce."

So he made a cunning trap by bending down a young tree just by the hole in the fence. He tied a rope to a high branch with a slip knot at the end, then he fixed this on to a stick.

Next time Brer Rabbit crept through the fence, he knocked the stick away, the rope caught him round the legs and the tree sprang back with Brer Rabbit dangling in the air.

"Oh, dear!" he cried, "I'm properly caught now!"

Just then, Brer Bear came along.

"What are you doing up there?" he asked.

"Making a pound a minute!" answered Brer Rabbit. "Brer Fox pays me to hang here and frighten the crows off his green peas and lettuce. But I'm very busy at present so, if you would like the job, you can take my place."

So Brer Bear helped Brer Rabbit down from the tree and fastened himself to a stronger part of the branch while Brer Rabbit ran away home with as much green stuff as he could carry.

"Ha! ha!" cried Brer Fox running
from his house with a big stick.
"So you're the thief who has been
stealing my green peas and lettuce!
Nicely caught Brer Bear!"

And poor Brer Bear got the punishment which should have
been for Brer Rabbit.

"It's not always the biggest people who have the best
brains," laughed Brer Rabbit as he enjoyed a meal of green
peas and lettuce.

BRER FOX
AND MRS. GOOSE

Mrs. Goose was down by the water doing her washing one day when Brer Fox passed along on the other side of the river.

"Ha, ha!" he muttered.

"That nice fat goose would make me a very nice supper. I'll creep into her house tonight when she is asleep and catch her."

He didn't know that Brer Rabbit was listening to his plan and, as soon as the fox was out of sight, Brer Rabbit hopped over the stepping-stones to warn Mrs. Goose.

"What shall I do?" wailed Mrs. Goose in a great flutter. "I can't escape from that dreadful Brer Fox if he breaks into my house," and she cried and cried and made her washing wetter and wetter.

"Just listen to me," said Brer Rabbit, who was always ready to play tricks on Brer Fox. "Make a bundle of your washing and put it in your bed, then fly up to the rafters and roost there for the night.

I'll have a chat with Brer Dog, he will help you."
So that night, Mrs. Goose did as Brer Rabbit had advised.

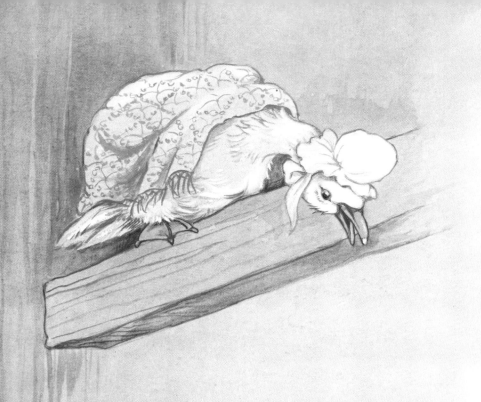

She made a big bundle of her washing and put it in her bed in a dark corner, then she flew up to the rafters and waited rather nervously to see what would happen.

Sure enough, at midnight, the door opened softly and Brer Fox crept in.

The room was so dark that it was easy to mistake the bundle of washing for a fine fat goose and Brer Fox, licking his lips, grabbed it and rushed out.

But Brer Dog was waiting for him and, if the fox hadn't dropped the bundle and run for his life, he would certainly have been caught.

The next morning the story went around that Brer Fox had tried to steal Mrs. Goose's washing!

All the animals laughed and laughed to think that the fine and cunning Brer Fox had wanted to steal anything so silly as Mrs. Goose's washing!

THE MOON IN THE POND

One evening when all the animals were feeling friendly, they decided to go fishing together.

But when they reached the pond, Brer Rabbit looked very worried.

"Look!" he cried. "The moon has fallen into the water. We won't catch any fish here until we have scooped it out."

So Brer Rabbit ran home to fetch a strong net.

"It seems to me," whispered Brer Fox, "that the moon is made of gold. I'm sure Brer Rabbit will try to keep it for himself so we mustn't let him get hold of it."

When Brer Rabbit came back with the net, Brer Fox took it from him.

"Let Brer Wolf and Brer Bear help me," he said. "You are too small to wade into the pond and pull that heavy moon from the water."

This was just what Brer Rabbit had planned so, while the big animals waded into the water, Brer Rabbit and his friend, Brer Tortoise, crept to the other side of the pond and started fishing.

Brer Fox, Brer Wolf and Brer Bear waded deeper and deeper into the water and tried to drag the net around the moon but, of course, as it was only the reflection of the moon, they couldn't catch it.

Then Brer Fox slipped and Brer Bear, stumbling over him, clutched Brer Wolf and they fell into the pond with a mighty splash!

When they had struggled back to the bank they saw Brer Rabbit and Brer Tortoise hurrying away with a basket of fine fish.

"Tricked again!" they growled.

BRER RABBIT
AND THE HONEY POT

Brer Rabbit was peeping through the grass one day when he saw Brer Bear walking down the road.

"I'll have a look inside Brer Bear's house," said the little rabbit, "there might be something nice to eat there."

He hopped along and, finding the door open, crept inside Brer Bear's house.

"Only bread and cheese on the table," grumbled Brer Rabbit. "I don't want that. I wonder what he keeps in the cupboard? Perhaps some lettuce or carrots or maybe a bag of oats."

Standing on a stool, Brer Rabbit opened the cupboard door.

"Nothing but cups and plates," muttered the rabbit, "except for that jar on the top shelf," and he stretched up a paw to reach it.

"Oh — oh!" over went the jar and out poured a stream of honey!

Poor Brer Rabbit was covered with sticky honey from head to foot and, although he licked and licked, it still stuck to him.

"Dear me!" he cried, "I like honey but not all over me! If I go out the bees will come after me and perhaps sting me if they think I've stolen their honey, and if I stay here Brer Bear will catch me."

At last he decided to run into the wood and roll in the leaves to rub off the honey.

This wasn't a very
good idea for the leaves
stuck to the honey and
made Brer Rabbit look
like a terrifying person.

But when he saw that the other animals
were frightened of him, he thought he might
be able to scare his old enemy, Brer Fox, so he
walked along waving his arms and making the
leaves give a peculiar "swishy" noise.

When Brer Bear saw him, he gave a howl and ran for
his life and didn't stop until he was safely home.
   The next animals Brer Rabbit met were Brer Fox
and Brer Wolf.
   They were busily making a plan to catch Brer Rabbit
and didn't see him until he jumped onto a hillock in
front of them.

"Gr — gr, I'm the Bogey Man!" shouted Brer Rabbit. "I eat bad wolves and foxes — I'll catch you both!"

"Help!" howled Brer Wolf, "Help!" barked Brer Fox, as Brer Rabbit shook his leaf-covered paws in the air — and off they ran!

It took Brer Rabbit a long time to clean off the honey but how he laughed! And every time he saw Brer Fox he shouted, "mind the Bogey Man doesn't get you!"

BRER WOLF BREAKS THE LAW

As Brer Rabbit was walking along one day, he was thinking as usual of what tricks he could play on Brer Fox and Brer Wolf but, this time, he was nearly caught himself.

"Help! help!" came a voice from nearby and Brer Rabbit saw that Brer Wolf had been trapped under a great boulder.

"Please help me!" cried the wolf. "Give the boulder a push and set me free."

So Brer Rabbit, feeling rather sorry for the wolf although he didn't really like him, gave the boulder a mighty heave and out crawled Brer Wolf.

But instead of thanking Brer Rabbit, Brer Wolf seized him by the ears and declared he would have rabbit pie for dinner that night.

"That's a fine way to say thank you," squeaked Brer Rabbit. "I'll never do you a good turn again as long as I live!"

"You certainly won't!" laughed Brer Wolf.

Then Brer Rabbit thought quickly.

"Of course, you know, Brer Wolf that it's breaking the law to kill anyone who rescues you?" he said.

"No, I didn't know that," answered Brer Wolf, doubtfully.

"Well," said Brer Rabbit, "we must ask Brer Tortoise. He's the expert on these matters. There'll be trouble for you if you are proved wrong."

So Brer Wolf agreed to go to Brer Tortoise's house.

Brer Tortoise looked very wise when they asked for his opinion but, luckily, he was a friend of Brer Rabbit and wanted to help him.

"This is a very difficult case," he said at last when both animals had explained what had happened, "but we must be certain that the law isn't broken. Before I can decide, I must see the scene where this took place."

So off went the three animals.

Brer Tortoise poked the boulder and walked around it.

"There is only one way to decide," he said to Brer Wolf. "I must see just how you were trapped."

So Brer Wolf crawled under the boulder and the tortoise and the rabbit rolled it over him.
Then Brer Tortoise said, "Brer Rabbit, you were wrong.

If you found Brer Wolf under that boulder he was minding his own business and you should have minded yours."
And Brer Tortoise and Brer Rabbit walked off and left Brer Wolf to be rescued by someone else.